© Copyright 1971 by Gakken Co., Ltd.
Published by Gakken Co., Ltd., Tokyo, Japan
First Japanese Publication, 1969
Distributed in the United States by
Silver Burdett Company, Morristown, New Jersey 07960
Library of Congress Catalog Card Number: 71-94810
Printed and bound in Japan

P. I. Tchaikovsky's
SWAN LAKE

illustrated by Shigeru Hatsuyama
adapted by Eriko Kishida
translated by Ann King Herring

Fantasia Pictorial
Stories from Famous Music

Gakken

Long, long ago, in a castle by a lake in the forest, there lived a young prince. His name was Siegfried.

One day the old princess, his mother, came to him and said, "Tomorrow, my son, you will be eighteen. In honor of your birthday, I have planned a grand ball. All the most beautiful girls will come as guests."

She paused and looked thoughtfully at Siegfried for a moment before going on. "And from among them, you must choose your bride."

In the evening, Siegfried and his friends went out through the forest to hunt. Soon they came to the lake. Its waters shone in the moonlight.

Suddenly, a flight of wild swans swooped downward out of the dark sky. As Siegfried fitted an arrow to his bowstring and quickly took aim, a single swan turned and flashed toward him. Upon its head, the swan wore a coronet of gold.

"Wait!"

A clear voice rang out. In the next instant, the swans had turned into a group of beautiful maidens.

"We are not really swans. We are human beings, just as you are. But an evil magician has cast a spell upon us, so that we can only return to our true form during the dark night," said the girl with the golden crown. "My name is Odette, and I am a princess from a land far away."

"When will the spell be broken?" Siegfried asked.

"Whenever and wherever a prince shall ask me to marry him. But he must be true in heart and in deed," she replied.

Siegfried took her hand in his. "At the ball tomorrow night, I must choose the one who is to be my bride. Now that I have seen you, how could I choose any other? Come to the ball, Odette. I shall not fail you."

Gazing happily into one another's eyes, they failed to see the dark shape that sat in a tree nearby, watching and listening. It was the magician, in the disguise of an owl.

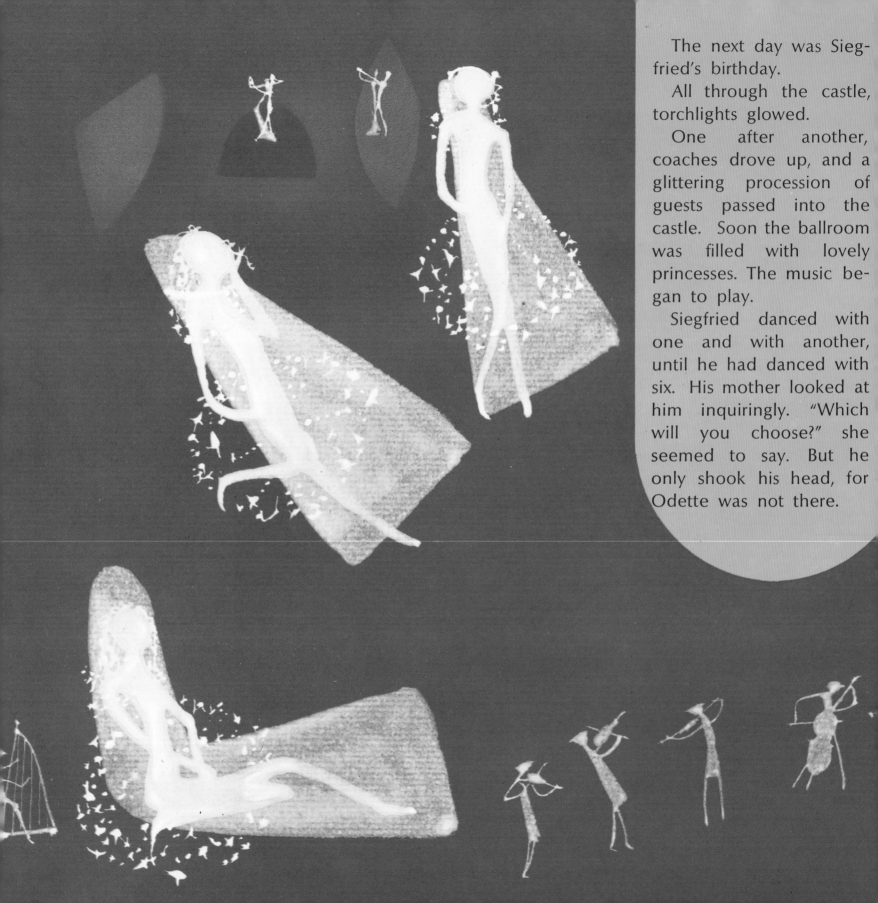

The next day was Siegfried's birthday.

All through the castle, torchlights glowed.

One after another, coaches drove up, and a glittering procession of guests passed into the castle. Soon the ballroom was filled with lovely princesses. The music began to play.

Siegfried danced with one and with another, until he had danced with six. His mother looked at him inquiringly. "Which will you choose?" she seemed to say. But he only shook his head, for Odette was not there.

At that moment, the trumpet sounded. Torches flickered low, and a chill wind blew through the hall as an elderly nobleman entered, leading with him a striking girl in a black gown. Siegfried gasped. "Odette!" he thought. "At last you have come."

Siegfried danced with the girl, and then he led her to his mother's chair and announced to all, "This is the one whom I have chosen."

"Music!" the guests shouted joyfully. "Music for Siegfried and his princess."

Then, from the darkness outside the ballroom windows, there came a rustle, like the beating of swan wings. Another voice spoke out.

"Siegfried! Here I am. That girl beside you is not Odette. The magician has tricked you, and you have failed me." The girl in black smiled a mocking smile, as the rustle of swan wings grew fainter and ceased altogether.

Siegfried glared at the nobleman in black.

"Who, then, are you?" Suddenly, all the lights flashed out, and an eerie blackness filled the hall. "Ha, ha! Don't you know who I am? And as for your bride-to-be, she is my own daughter," the magician gloated. "I have triumphed over you. Now you will never set Odette free."

He laughed wickedly, and swept out of the room.

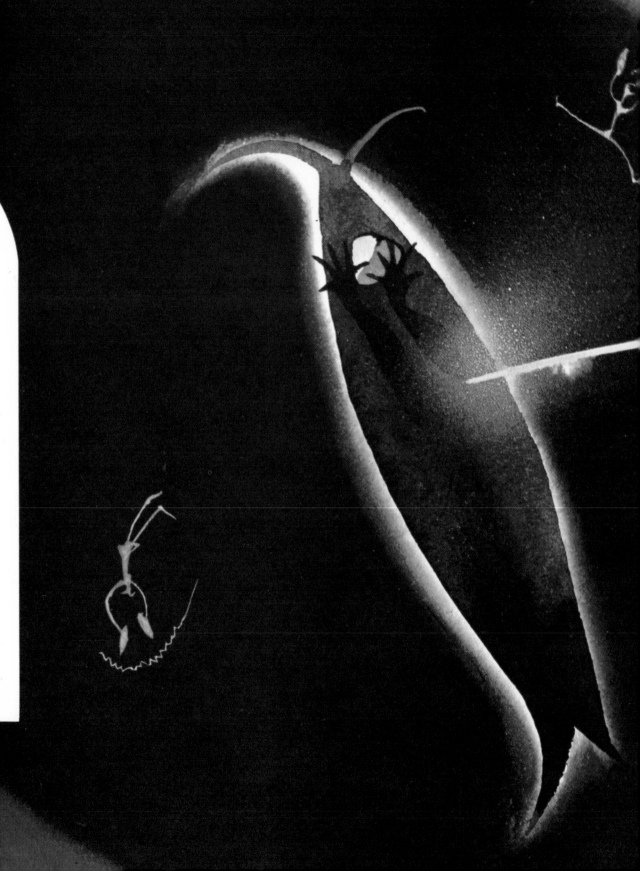

Drawing his sword, Siegfried rushed after the magician. "Odette," he cried. "Forgive me. I must and I will set you free. Die, vile sorcerer!"

The young prince attacked so fiercely that the magician was taken by surprise. But as he fell, mortally wounded, he looked at Siegfried and laughed.

"Faithless fool, despair! Even though you kill me, still you can never break the spell," the magician shrieked, with his last breath.

Alone, Siegfried ran out into the night.

At midnight by the lake shore, a faint echo of ringing bells drifted across the water as the swan maidens waited for Odette. They spoke in whispers.

"When she returns, surely she will bring the prince with her."

"The two of them will be married soon, and then we shall all be free forever."

But Odette came back alone. With tears in her voice, she spoke.

"Try to be brave, and do not weep. I was too late. The prince has chosen the magician's daughter. For us, there is no hope left."

At that moment, Siegfried ran up.

"Odette!" he pleaded. "Listen to me. I have killed the magician!"

But Odette only wept.

"I thank you for that, Siegfried. But still the spell cannot be broken."

"Why?"

"Do you not know? Because you have broken your promise to me, and chosen the magician's daughter."

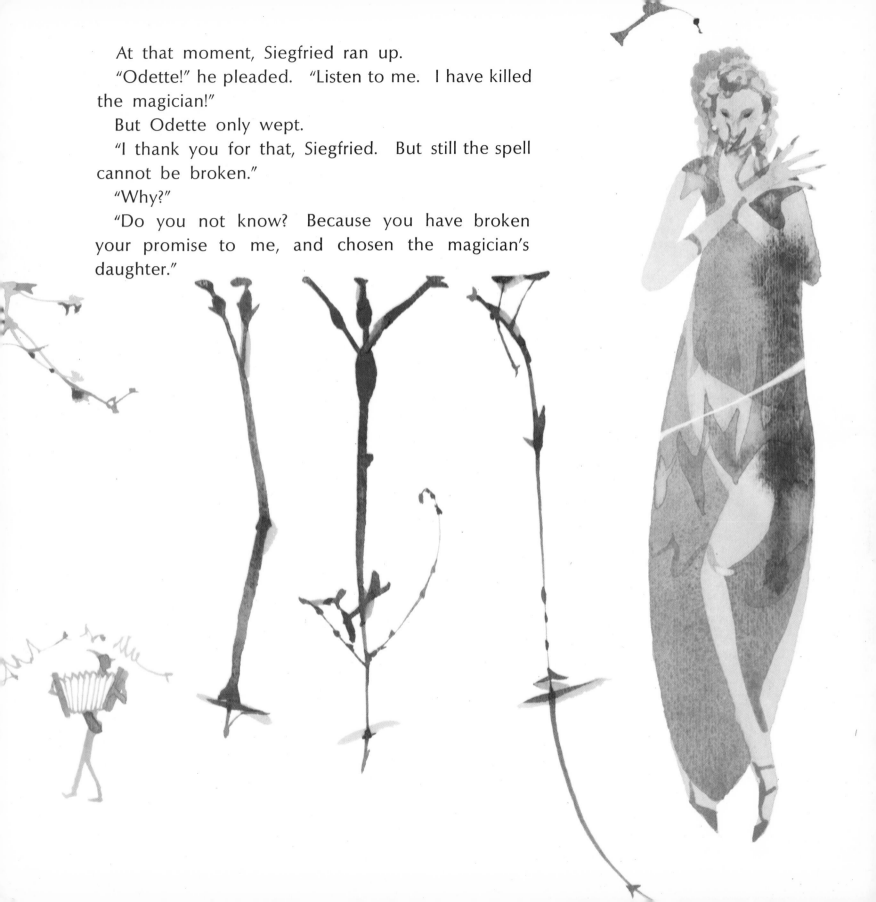

"Now we shall never be free. Siegfried, farewell!"
Despairing, she ran toward the lake and threw
herself into the water.

"Odette, wait! Wherever you go, I will go with
you, for I love no one else but you."

He seized her hand, and together they sank into
the depths of the lake.

On the bank, the swan maidens knelt, as they
watched the dark waters sadly.

Even as the swan maidens watched, a golden haze shimmered up out of the waters. A single beam of moonlight streamed down to meet it. Where haze and moonlight met, two bright figures stood— Odette and Siegfried, dressed in bridal white and silver and crowned with stars. The moonbeam led them upward toward a radiant world of light, where they would be together forever. The watchers' sorrow turned to joyful gratitude, for they knew that now the spell was broken. When dawn came, the swan maidens were free.